SILVERSTONE STORIES

Lauren -

This is my family written with love.

Judy

2009

SILVERSTONE STORIES

& Other Mishagos

A Retrospective of
Siblings Times Ten

Judith L. White

Eshel
Books
Washington • Baltimore

ISBN 13: 978-0-910155-69-4

Library of Congress control number: 2006935919

ESHEL BOOKS
An imprint of Bartleby Press
9045 Maier Road, Suite D
Laurel, MD 20723
800-953-9929
www.EshelBooks.com

In memory of the following grandchildren of
Rabbi Gedaliah and Rebitzen Rebecca
Mayer Silverman
Mortimer Silverman
Robin Shrager Gerson
Joan Shapiro
Lisa Sterling
Howard Shrager
Doreen Hurwitz Brown
Elwood Silverstone

CONTENTS

FOREWORD

M ore than twenty years ago, Letty Cottin Pogrebin, described family in words which still resonate for us:

> *"The family endures because it offers the truth of mortality and immortality within the same group. The family endures because ... it seems to individualize and socialize its children, to make us feel at the same time unique and yet joined to all humanity, accepted as is and yet challenged to grow, loved unconditionally and yet propelled by greater expectations. Only in the family can so many extremes be reconciled and synthesized. Only in the family do we have a lifetime in which to do it."**

Silverstone Stories & Other Mishagos: A Retrospective of Siblings Times Ten, Judith Becker-White's lovingly created portrait of her own large extended family, evokes those truths of family life. Raised in the warm embrace of her mother's orthodox Jewish family, Dr. Becker-White's experience was unique, but no matter the ethnicity or religion, her story of

---

Family Politics: Love and Power on an Intimate Frontier McGraw-Hill 1983.

one large American family is familiar to all of us. As you get to know her grandparents and the ten children they raised early in the twentieth century in Washington, D.C., no doubt you will think of your own family.

You will meet Gedaliah Silverstone, an orthodox rabbi who after he emigrated here from England and Ireland, founded Tifereth Israel synagogue and the Washington Hebrew Home, institutions that thrive today. Rabbi Gedaliah published many scholarly books, but you will be impressed with much more than his accomplishments. You will get to know a gentle man, one who was willing to bend the strictures of his orthodoxy to make others comfortable. You will get to know a charitable man, one who gave back a gift of money he needed and asked that it be used to start a home for the aging.

You will meet the rabbi's wife, Rebecca, a woman of great charm and wit who indeed made each of her ten children feel unique, who loved them all unconditionally, and whose house was always open to other relatives. You will find out that even so pious a woman invested in real estate and sold "ceremonial wine" in her basement during prohibition to earn money for the family.

And you will meet, in turn, each of the ten Silverstones — five sisters who, although constrained by the expectations of women during that period, were all adventurous and five brothers who pursued diverse careers. As you chuckle over the many, amusing Silverstone tales, you will recognize those stories for what they are, the ones we talk about with our own family when we are reminiscing, the stories our children will tell to their children, the ones that always start "remember when..." and become part of our family lore.

Dr. White's family memoir does more than document her own fond memories and deep connection to an extended international network of aunts, uncles and cousins. With humor and gentle self-mocking, she brings to life the rich tapestry of one remarkable family living through an extraordinary time and evokes our own sense of what family means to us.

In our country, where wave after wave of immigrants have reinvented themselves, many of us have become interested in who makes up our own family history. Whether our ties are to groups that came to a newly discovered continent to practice their religion freely or to slaves brought here under the most horrendous circumstances and forced to give up their freedom, we want to know what our roots are. In our modern, technological country, where moving so far from family is often the norm, many of us are finding new ways to connect with cousins we may never have met or to keep in touch with folks we see only during reunions. Whatever your own ties may be, this portrait of the extended Silverstone family will evoke the power, pleasure and strength of family and connection.

I. King Jordan, Ph.D.
President
Gallaudet University

PREFACE

This book has been ten years in the making. The draft was started in 1995 in anticipation of my uncle Rabbi Harry's one-hundredth birthday celebration. But not until my mother, Mirm, died in 2000 did I find the documentation to support the many Silverstone stories I heard while growing up.

I wanted to share these stories to preserve the charm and antics of the ten Silverstone siblings who, although reared in a true, orthodox Jewish environment, were given the opportunity to be free spirits and follow their dreams. Embedded in these stories are insights into the culture and traditions of the Jewish religion.

Hopefully, readers will be encouraged to collect stories and documents from their own family history so that they may pass on to future generations the styles and customs of their heritage.

This retrospective begins in the late 1800's. My grandmother, Rebecca Baker, married a young rabbi named Gedaliah (Gedaly) Silverstone in December 1892 in Liverpool, England. It was an elegant affair with dinner at 5PM and a ball at eight.

Wedding Invitation - 1892

Rabbi Gedaliah was the twelfth in a line of rabbis in his family. Gedaliah's father was Rabbi Joshua Meir Silverstone of Liverpool, England. Gedaliah's son, Harry, became the 13th in the line of rabbis. And it was here that the Silverstone rabbinical lineage stopped.

My grandmother, Rebitzen Rebecca Baker Silverstone, known as "Ma" was from London, England. Her family also came from a long line of rabbis and she had a bachelor brother named Joe Baker who was a Barrister under the English legal system. He visited Washington, D.C. in 1957 and my fiancé and I were fortunate to spend time with him.

We started a wonderful correspondence after Joe Baker

RSVP Card - 1892

returned home but, unfortunately, he died in 1959 and I never had the chance to visit with him again.

Rabbi Gedaliah and his wife Rebitzen Rebecca lived in several countries, moving from England to Ireland to America to *Eretz Israel*, the "land of Israel," as Palestine was referred to by Jews before the State of Israel was founded. Rabbi Gedaliah led congregations in Belfast, Ireland and in Washington, D.C. It was his brogue that earned him the nickname 'the Irish Rabbi.' Together, they reared ten children, five boys and five girls. In her later years, when doctors would ask my Bubbie Rebecca how many children she had, she would only admit to five girls, her reason being that if she said she had five girls *and* five boys, the doctors would think she was too old and would not pay proper attention to her.

Some of the stories in this retrospective may appear to be slightly exaggerated. My mother explained to me that with ten siblings in the family, the only way for any child to get his or her mother's attention was to embellish the truth. These stories have been told over and over again by various Silverstone siblings, with all the important details remaining the same. From my personal experience with my nine Silverstone aunts and uncles, with whom I was close, there is more truth than fiction in these stories.

When I was a young girl in the mid 1940s, my mother used to force me to eat all my food "because of all the starving children in Europe". I was presented spoonful after spoonful for each of our relatives. Never did she repeat a relative's name during the same meal, yet the names went on forever. No family could ever be this large! But as I grew older and met the extended Silverstone family, I learned that the Silverstone family really is *that* large. And today, with the advent of email, cell phones and easy air travel, we are able to keep in touch, visiting often and continuing the Silverstone legacy.

As the Silverstone children became adults they fudged about their ages, but the birth order is as follows:

Dorothy
Anna
Harry
Ellis, alias Bobsy
Elizabeth/Besse
Rose
Joseph/Joe
Herbert/Herbie
Philip/Phil
Miriam/Mirm (my mother)

The ten Silverstone children were close, enjoying each other's company and continuing throughout their lives to do funny things. These memories remain bright and contribute to *Silverstone Stories and Other Mishagos.*

AND SO THE STORIES BEGIN...

ACKNOWLEDGEMENTS

M ost important is my gratitude to my husband Len, who has been my partner since high school. He was, and is, a constant support in this project. His patience and guidance in making the necessary computer moves will not be forgotten.

Peter Porosky, editor, saw potential in a very basic draft. His knowledge and suggestions brought my manuscript, after several revisions over as many years, to its present form. I am grateful that he had faith in my efforts.

Laura Lopez-Cayzedo offered incredible insights. She read and re-read this retrospective so many times that she feels she knows my family even though she has never met any of the Silverstones.

Chapter 1
RABBI GEDALIAH

The father of the ten Silverstone children was my grand-father Rabbi Gedaliah, known by his family as "Da." A scholar and a prolific writer, he published thirty-eight books and spent his days studying and debating interpretations of the *Torah* and *Talmud* with other rabbinical scholars.

Rabbi Gedaliah Silverstone

He was a tall, imposing man who showed both grace and tolerance to balance his orthodoxy. In true Orthodox tradition, an observant Jewish man is not to touch a woman to whom he is not related. I am told that my grandfather, a gentleman, never refused to shake a woman's hand if she unknowingly offered it to him. Also, Rabbi Gedaliah would always partake of a piece of fruit, an orange, a banana, when visiting a home that may not be *kosher*. His reasoning was that it would be impolite to refuse a woman's hand or a hostess's gesture of hospitality when either was offered with the best of intentions.

*Rabbi Gedaliah, seated third from the left,
and rabbis studying the Talmud.*

Simcha Torah is traditionally a happy holiday when people express their joy by singing and dancing with the Torah. Da was known to remark that he would be happier if people studied more and danced less.

My cousin Elinore, Besse's daughter, fondly recalls that when Gedaliah saw his grandchildren he would give each one a gold coin and a pat on the tush.

In his diary, Grandfather Gedaliah wrote that in 1901 he was paid one hundred dollars per month to be the Rabbi in the City of Belfast. "Realizing that $100.00 a month was too meager a pay for a rabbi with eight children," he left the Irish rabbinate and traveled to America.

"I accepted a rabbinical position in the capitol city of Washington, D.C. with great honor," he wrote, "and I remained there for thiry years. In the city of Washington, D.C., I published some thirty-one books and it made a great impression on rabbinic scholars and researchers."

During his time in Washington, Rabbi Gedaliah was a principle founder and leader of Tifereth Israel Synagogue, which was originally located at 14th and Euclid Streets, NW. He was succeeded as rabbi in the congregation by his son, Rabbi Harry. Today, this synagogue has an active congregation on 16th Street, NW.

One "Da" story is referred to as the "New York Breeze." It is still being debated whether it was son Joe or son Ellis who traveled with Da to New York. It makes no difference. The logic, or lack thereof, behind this story is still enchanting. We'll say it was Joe. Joe was often asked to drive Rabbi Gedaliah to New York on business. On this trip, they checked into the Broadway Central Hotel. The temperature was in

News article of Women's Group from Tifereth Israel Synagogue Washington, D.C., November 18, 1928

the high 90s and hotels at that time did not have air con-
ditioning. The two men went to their room, opened the
window, and lay down in the darkened room to go to sleep.
Da found the heat oppressive. No air was stirring and Da
could barely breathe. He called to Joe in the next bed and
asked that he open the door to the hallway.

"Maybe that way," he said, "we could create a breeze."
Joe, too hot and tired to move, and thinking that it would
not be safe to sleep with the hallway door open, said O.K.
and opened the nearby closet door. On hearing a door open,
Da took a deep breath and sighed, "Ahh. What a *michayah,*
that feels better already."

Da dressed up in his silk top hat and white gloves to
attend President Taft's wedding anniversary celebration. He
joined the Archbishop of Washington, D.C. at one of the
banquet tables. Mrs. Taft approached Rabbi Gedaliah and

*Rabbi Gedaliah (Front Row, 5th from right) with President
Coolidge at the 12th Annual Mizrachi Convention in front of
White House. 1926*

asked why he was not eating, assuring him that all the food was kosher. Then the Archbishop asked why the Rabbi was so old-fashioned about eating pork.

"I promise you," replied Rabbi Gedaliah, "when you celebrate your marriage, I will eat pork."

In 1937, Da decided to retire and return to Palestine. It was of utmost importance to Da that when he died, it would be in the Holy Land. The story in the *Talmud* states that when the Messiah comes, he will first appear on Mount Scopus. Thus, my grandfather insisted that he must be in Palestine when he died so that he, too, could be buried on Mount Scopus. Ma thought this was *meshuganah*. She said they owed everyone in town and had no money to travel.

Da, as always, said not to worry, "God will provide." Ma confided this dilemma to her good friend, Mrs. Wexler.

"How can we go to Palestine now when we owe everyone in town?"

A big farewell dinner was planned to honor Rabbi Gedaliah and his Rebitzen. A very large amount of money was raised as a farewell gift and presented to Da at the dinner. As Mrs. Wexler's son-in-law handed Da the money in a sealed envelope, Ma gave a sigh of relief.

"At last we will have the money to pay all our debts before we leave town."

Da accepted the envelope and, without even opening it, turned and presented this gift back to the *Shul* president, stating that he wanted the money to be used to start a new Hebrew Home on Spring Street in northwest Washington, D.C. The Hebrew Home of Greater Washington is now a major resource and nursing home for the Washington metropolitan Jewish community and is located in Rockville, Maryland.

Ma had a fit. No one ever knew how much money was in that envelope. Somehow, however, God did provide. They paid their debts, Ma complied with Da's wishes, and they left their family in the United States, traveling to Palestine in 1937.

You might wonder how a father of ten, with nine of his children living in Washington, D.C., could be so emphatic about moving to Palestine. One can only surmise that his strong religious principles formed his decision that he must be in Palestine at the time of his death.

Newspaper notification of Rabbi Gedaliah's relocation to Palestine to live out the rest of his life. 1937

For the next seven years in Palestine, life was rich and full. This was evidenced by the letters Ma continuously wrote

<table>
<tr><td>

RABBI

G. SILVERSTONE

RABBI OF WASHINGTON

R E H A V I A

IBN-SHAPRUT STREET 19

DR. BUXBAUM'S HOUSE

</td><td>

ה ר ב

גדלי" סילווערסטאן

הרב דוואאש'ונגטאן

רחביה

רחוב אבן שפרוט 19

בית ד"ר פ. בוקסבוים

</td></tr>
</table>

to each of their children. My mother preserved these letters which were written on Da's stationery with his printed letterhead. His letterhead showed that his heart was still in Washington, D.C. noting "Rabbi of Washington."

Every letter to my mother began with "My dear Miriam and Sam! I hope this will find you in the best of health," and always ended with the salutation, "Da sends his love to all of you." But Da never wrote directly to any of his ten children.

Even with the advent of World War II, the contents of Ma's letters contained family gossip and told of their activities in Palestine; friends who visited and religious traditions that were carried out. Overlooking the hardships the War brought, Ma's concern was that her daughters in America had enough household help so that they wouldn't work too hard and that her grandchildren were getting the proper amount of meat and vegetables.

Another of Ma's concerns was the custom of buying new clothes for the family at *Passover* time. This refers to the tradition, the Hebrew word being *minhac*, of having something new, *shehecheyanu*. The *Shehecheyan, a* prayer of thanks, refers to the "first" of everything new for each season and expresses personal gratitude for good health and having been able to reach this day. In several of her letters, Ma would remind her daughters to buy new clothes for their family so that they would look their best at the Passover services at the synagogue.

In one letter, written in October 1938, Ma reports that daughter Dolly had spoken with the American Consulate to make arrangements for Ma and Da to move to England.

Ma's reply was, "believe me; I have no intention of leaving Palestine; not even for the King of England. I am so comfortable and content here that I would not think of it." Ma still owned apartment buildings and houses in Washington, D.C. and was receiving revenue from the renters who lived there. Rabbi Gedaliah was a scholar and a dreamer. The family joke was that, although he would get a weekly salary check from the Tifereth Israel Synagogue, he gave his money away before he got home. Rebetizin Rebecca was the practical wife. She took care of the family's finances, making extra money by selling "ceremonial wine" during the prohibition years. As each of their children married, money was sent to Ma. She wisely invested in rental properties in Washington, D.C., and secured their retirement years.

Ma often showed her delightful sense of humor in her letters as well. "Don't wait for me to send photos because everyone tells me I'm getting better looking everyday, so I'll wait until I get really good looking."

On November 16, 1938, Ma wrote to reassure her family, "When you read about Palestine, remember that the Arabs are not in the New City where we live. The English soldiers are taking care of them now." She then went on to express how much she wished she had access to a telephone and was able to call the States.

In letters written in the winter of 1939, Ma complained about the money Da spent printing newer editions of the books he had written. On April 16, 1939, Ma thanked my mother for the $10.00 for Da that she had enclosed in her letter, noting that "it was nine and a half too much because he will use the money to print other books."

She also wrote, in her lightly veiled code, that the heat they had in their apartment would be good if it were summertime, but they could not move because in Palestine they had to sign a lease for a year's rental. They often used the heat from their oven in an effort to warm up their apartment.

Ma noted that she checked with their local post office because she was worried that sending a letter with Yiddish or Hebrew writing might get her into trouble. "The people at the post office assured me that it was not a problem."

In June of 1939, Ma wrote that Da was doing well. "He is not so busy with weddings and can relax more. The weather is warm and a housekeeper still comes three times a week to help with the cleaning and laundry." Again, Ma reminded my mother that she, too, should have daily household help for cleaning, cooking and childcare.

Ma responded to Mirm's invitation in July, 1939 to visit the family in Washington by saying that they had absolutely no intention of traveling to America, as they were very comfortable in Palestine, and expressed the hope that, in the near future, the family would travel to visit them.

"You may read in the papers that there is trouble in Haifa, but Haifa is far from Jerusalem and everything is safe here. Also, you must remind the family that we are older than they are and, therefore, they must travel here to see us."

"Dolly keeps sending me dresses, coats and hats from London and Paris. Please tell her to stop sending me clothes as the duty is very high when I have to retrieve those items here."

The following week, July 20, she wrote about the news of trouble in Jaffa where many Arabs were killed. The people in Jerusalem are, "getting very quiet and hope that Hitler will stop fighting." This was Ma's first reference to their concerns about the war, the impact it might have on Palestine, and expressing, "I wish I was back in Washington, D.C." As always, she signed her letter, "Love to everybody. Mother," with the added note, "Da sends his love to all of you."

In letters dated July 1939, Ma writes that she is concerned about the hot weather in D.C. and that she doesn't have a telephone as some of her friends do, but that they get all the news over the radio. Also, that they are safe because, "the English soldiers frighten all the Arabs away."

August 1939: "I'm sure you received my postcard from Tel-Aviv. I was surprised to see that Tel-Aviv looks so nice and modern. Everything looks beautiful and I think I will go back again next week."

August 30, 1939 revealed Ma's concerns about her real estate holdings in Washington, D.C. for the first time. She asked if the renters were paying on time and if the taxes were paid. "I would like to sell one house if it is possible, but I wouldn't take less than $6,000.00. You know Da, he would take ten dollars for all of it. I hope it would not take very long before it will sell."

September 1939 and the High Holidays were approaching. Ma's letters then expressed her worry about whether my mother would be able to leave her young children at home to go to services at the *shul* for *Yom Tov*. On a lighter note, Ma wrote that she had made some new friends from America and England, and was going into the *Shadchen* business, trying to make a marriage between two of them. "Love to all the family and tell them I wish them a happy new year."

September 25, 1939 again reveals Ma's sense of humor. She writes that she hopes next year, "things will quiet down and all the children will come to Palestine to visit. Da said not to write that invitation because all the children in D.C. will ask for a key to our house in Palestine."

In October 1939, Ma writes that, "the weather is turning cold. Mail delivery is very slow, sometimes only once a week. And it takes much longer to get letters from Palestine, so don't worry if you don't get letters on time." She inquires about her other nine children, their spouses, and all the gossip between them. She also notes that, "Da is on a diet and won't eat meat. [I don't know if this is a fact or one of Ma's lightly veiled codes meaning, 'no meat available.']"

"We hear the news on the radio everyday and it is not good. I hope we will be able to hear good news soon. I did have a luncheon party in my house and made everything the same like I did in America as I did not want to lose my good name and our guests have not stopped talking about that."

In letters dated 1940, Ma wrote that, "everything is quiet

here and the Arabs are behaving. Da is feeling much better, but says that if he could see all his grandchildren he would feel even better." She inquired about the lives of all the Silverstone children and grandchildren, their houses, their household help, and about her American real estate holdings. She also wrote that she was happy her daughter Anna and Anna's family were now living in Washington because Marseille, France was not a good place to be at the time.

As the war intensified, the tone of Ma's letters changed. In 1941 she comments that, "the heat they give us here in our apartment is a joke. They call this a heated apartment, but it is much colder here in Jerusalem than in Tel Aviv. Da doesn't want to move and the people here are very nice to me because they think I come from America and have a lot of money. When you come to visit, come in the winter, as Palestine has the best oranges which you have never seen before; you get them so cheap that it pays you to come here.

"My passport was 'operated' on. They cut it. I had to tell the Government how rich I am and to give them the addresses of my properties in America. My apartment this year is worse than last year. If it were not for the kindness of the Government we would live on the mountains and get good fresh air. We also get plenty of fresh air in our apartment. Pesach will be very cold. Everybody is having trouble getting matzah. I hope that next year will be better for everybody. They are not building any houses or apartments now. Dolly [living in London] doesn't send letters now, only checks. When the war stops, Da is coming to see your house and all his grandchildren. Your envelopes are too heavy for air-mail. It took four months for your last letter to arrive."

Letters in 1943 bring news that the money the family sends comes in handy, the weather is very cold, and food is scarce. Ma had to go early in the morning to get the staples that they needed. "We are short of a lot of things. My doctor doesn't believe my age, but I feel it. We won't be going away this summer as Da doesn't like to leave the house. Da thinks the best and cheapest hotel is home."

In the summer of 1943, Ma wrote, "Many things are difficult to get here now. We don't ask the price of things, we ask if we can get them. I'm sorry I did not buy last year what I need this year as I can't get what I need. Here everybody is going without stockings. Please send me some as I am too old to be in style. We did go to Bat Yam, where it is cooler, and we got a good rest and now we feel much better. Da is getting massages now and is feeling a little better."

In August 1943 Ma confirmed that she received Mirm's letters from June. "The mailman is very good to me and gives me all my mail at one time."

"I sent you a Happy New Year's card for this September. I hope you receive it before *Pesach* in April."

Throughout 1943, her letters described how the living conditions were becoming more difficult in Palestine, with most of the emphasis on the scarcity of food.

"We can't get vegetables here. I wish I could come to your garden and help myself to the vegetables. If the family in America want to lose weight, they should come to Palestine. If people get high blood pressure from eating meat, nobody would suffer from high blood pressure in my town. We now have heat in our apartment because a neighbor from

London fixed our heat. Please don't send your children to school when it is cold."

"I went to Tel Aviv to see a specialist. When the doctor saw me so weak he got a shock; but on the other hand, when I saw the amount I had to pay for my visit, I got a shock."

Over the years, Ma would convey information about one sibling to another; she wasn't shy about expressing her opinion. In one letter Ma wrote how happy she was that I was born a girl. "You know that I like daughters more than sons."

Still, Ma expressed her concerns about the well-being of her children. "How can you manage with a maid only three times a week? How can you get out in the evenings when you have no maid? Also, I think our youngest son,

The notification of Rabbi Gedaliah Silverstone's death was pasted on bulletin boards and walls in Israel.

Philip, doesn't have good sense. Ask your husband, Dr. Sam Becker, if Phil is curable for getting brains."

Ma was also worried about her son, Rabbi Harry, and his position in the synagogue. "It is more important to keep a position at work than to be busy printing books."

A letter in February 1944 sent news that Da did not feel well and had agreed to go to the doctor. "He talks so slowly I can't hear him. He is not excited anymore."

Rabbi Gedaliah Silverstone died in July 1944 in Jerusalem, Palestine. He never was able to see any of his ten children again, and of course I never met my grandfather Rabbi Gedaliah Silverstone.

The notification of Rebbe Gedaliah Silverstone's death was pasted on bulletin boards and walls in Israel. The wording is old-style religious Hebrew and states:

> The 'Ohel Torah' House of David Yeshiva announces, with great sorrow, the passing of its vice president. The great scholar Rabbi Gedaliah Silverstone (The memory of a good man is blessed.) The funeral will take place on Sunday, the third of Av at 11 am from his dwelling on 19 Ibn Shapbrut Street, the house of Dr. Boxbaum. All who are dear to the Torah are requested to pay their respects to the honorable deceased and to attend the funeral.
>
> —The Management and the Rabbinate Association*

Like many orthodox Jewish men, Rabbi Gedaliah felt compelled to be in Jerusalem when he died so that he could be buried on the Mount of Olives, also known as Mount

---

*Translation by Sam Bergman

Scopus. From this site, the view of the Old City is spectacular. But most importantly, orthodox men believe Zechariah's prophecy in the Old Testament that says that when the "end of days" are upon us, this is where the Messiah will appear.

Rabbi Gedaliah Silverstone's Tombstone

The tradition says that when the Messiah arrives, all the dead men will be resurrected and those men buried at this site will be the first to rise from the dead.

Because of the holiness of this site, orthodox Jews insisted that women not be permitted on this burial ground. During the war of 1948, the Mount of Olives was in Jordanian hands. The Jordanian people took the stones of ancient tombs and used them for construction purposes.

In 1967, Israel reclaimed this area and women were no longer excluded from visiting the cemetery. Fortunately,

10 B   THE WASHINGTON POST
Wednesday, July 26, 1944

District Rabbi 35 Years Dies In Jerusalem

Noted Rabbi Is Dead

Chief Rabbi Gedalia George Silverstone, 75, who led the Jewish community of Washington for 35 years until his departure for Palestine 8 years ago, died Saturday in Jerusalem, his family here learned yesterday.

They were advised by cable that Chief Rabbi Isaac Hertzog of Palestine conducted funeral services Sunday.

Rabbi Silverstone, for many years a vice president of the Union of Orthodox Rabbis of America, was the author of some 60 textbooks of Rabbinical law.

A native of Sakot, Russia, and son of a rabbi, he was graduated from the famed Rabbinical School at Telz and then went to Belfast, Ireland. In 1905, he came to America and took over the pulpit in Washington. He was succeeded by his son, Rabbi Harry Silverstone.

He also leaves four other sons, Ellis, Herbert, Joseph and Philip Silverstone, all of Washington, and five daughters, Mrs. Nathan Hurwitz, Mrs. Nathan Shapiro and Mrs. Samuel Becker of Washington; Mrs. Conrad Silverman of London, England, and Mrs. Herman Schrager of Plainfield, N. J.

Among his grandchildren are Capt. Mortimer Silverman of the British army, adjutant to Foreign Secretary Anthony Eden, and Pvt. Elwood Silverstone and Sergt. Myron Hurwitz, both serving with the American forces in France.

Rev. Gedaliah Silverstone

brother, Maddox Trenholm of 1332 H st. nw.

Funeral arrangements will not be made until word is received from C[...] ing ove[...]

Newspaper Article Announcing Rabbi Silverstone's Death, July 26, 1944

Grandfather Gedaliah's tomb stone was recovered and repaired using money contributed by the Silverstone family's congregation Bet Gedaliah. Presently, his grave site on the Mount of Olives rests three levels below the road that separates the King David Hotel and the cemetery. There are an estimated 150,000 graves on the Mount, including many prominent rabbis and other famous people, such as David Ben-Gurion, who is considered the founding father of the State of Israel and was its first prime minister.

Whenever Silverstones visit Jerusalem, they are sure to visit Gedaliah's grave and place a stone on his tombstone in order to let him know someone was there and thinking of him, as is the Jewish tradition. Over the years, several of Gedaliah's grandchildren and great-grandchildren have visited the cemetery on Mount Scopus and searched for his tombstone. Unable to read Hebrew, they placed stones on the tombstones they thought were Gedaliah's. Photographs taken at the time show that the Silverstone relatives have made some other grandfathers very happy.

Ma did not want to leave Palestine, but in 1945, she fell and broke her arm. Multiple discussions were held in my house and it was determined that she could not live alone in Palestine and that Joe, the toughest of the brothers, should fly to Palestine and bring Ma home to Washington, D.C., where her family could take care of her. An entourage of Silverstones accompanied Joe to Union Station, where he took the train to New York and from there boarded the airplane for Palestine. In 1945 this was a major undertaking. Joe flew to Palestine and convinced Ma to return to the states with him. They packed up her belongings, settled her business concerns, and flew 'home'. She lived in an apartment five minutes from her children. A wonderful woman was hired to live with Ma as a companion, and her children visited everyday. Dr. Sam *never* missed a daily visit with Ma. She died in her apartment surrounded by family in November 1957.

Chapter 2
REBITZEN REBECCA

Rebitzen Rebecca (Ma), the Rabbi's wife, was a small, beautiful woman with a wonderful sense of humor. She invested in real estate to help support the family, and also made some extra 'pin' money by surreptitiously selling 'ceremonial wine' from their basement during Prohibition.

With ten children living together in a house, one would expect total chaos. But when I talked with my aunts and uncles about their childhood, each expressed the feeling that Ma made him or her feel that he or she was the favorite. When not working on her real estate holdings, Ma could usually be found in the kitchen. She had a housekeeper/cook to help her and would prepare a different meal for each child, catering to each one's specific taste. In addition to the ten children, there always seemed to be extra cousins or visiting relatives living at the house at one time or another. While their father was busy with his congregation and daily debates over Torah interpretations with other rabbis and scholars, Ma worked her magic in a quiet, mystical way.

Following orthodox tradition, Ma wore a *shadel*. A *shadel* is a wig, often made of human hair, which an (observant) orthodox woman would wear when she left her home and went out in public. Besse, one of my mother's older sisters, had gone on a date one night and arrived home way past her curfew. Not daring to turn on a light, Besse snuck into the house and made her way up the stairs. She put her hand on the base of the banister and grabbed a handful of human hair. I can picture the histrionics that must have caused. Lights flew on and everyone ran into the hallway to see what the blood-curdling scream was about. Besse had grabbed her mother's *shadel...* so much for sneaking in after curfew.

This next story concerns the notification from my grandmother of the death of her beloved husband, Gedaliah. I was told many, many times that in July 1944, a cablegram was sent to my Uncle Joe's house informing the family, in very few words, of Gedaliah's death, with the added directive "DON'T TELL MIRYAM." This seemed like a good story, illustrating how one might want to protect the baby of the family from sad news, but I never believed it. In such a close-knit family, one wonders how long this information could be kept secret and toward what end. Then in 1995, I was going through some old papers and, lo and behold, there was the original cablegram from Jerusalem inscribed with the words, "DON'T TELL MIRYAM." Finding this cable-gram was a motivating force in my desire to write *Silverstone Stories and Other Mishagos.*

The winters were cold in Washington, D.C., so Ma used to spend them with a companion in Miami Beach, Florida. One winter, Mirm and Besse accompanied Ma to Florida, but were quickly bored because the place where Ma stayed accommodated so many old people. One night, Mirm and

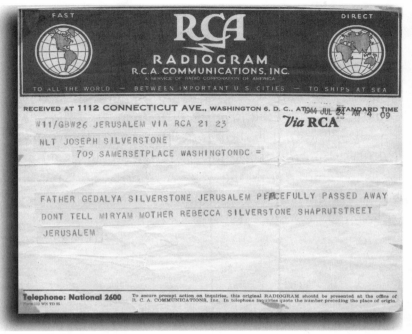

FAST   DIRECT

RCA
RADIOGRAM
R.C.A. COMMUNICATIONS, INC.
A SERVICE OF RADIO CORPORATION OF AMERICA

TO ALL THE WORLD — BETWEEN IMPORTANT U.S. CITIES — TO SHIPS AT SEA

RECEIVED AT 1112 CONNECTICUT AVE., WASHINGTON 6, D. C., AT 1944 JUL 24 AM 4 09 STANDARD TIME

W11/GBW26 JERUSALEM VIA RCA 21 23   *Via* RCA

NLT JOSEPH SILVERSTONE
      709 SAMERSETPLACE WASHINGTONDC =

FATHER GEDALYA SILVERSTONE JERUSALEM PEACEFULLY PASSED AWAY
DONT TELL MIRYAM MOTHER REBECCA SILVERSTONE SHAPRUTSTREET
JERUSALEM

Telephone: National 2600   To secure prompt action on inquiries, this original RADIOGRAM should be presented at the office of R. C. A. COMMUNICATIONS, Inc. In telephone inquiries quote the number preceding the place of origin.

Cablegram 1944

Besse returned from a day on the beach, and Ma told them that to cheer them up she had invited two young men over for the evening. Mirm and Besse made a beeline to their bedroom to fix their make-up and hair and put on their most appealing outfits. When the two young men arrived they turned out to be Asa Yolson*, the father of singer Al Jolson and his friend, old man Reverend Goldman.

Ma had never been to a nightclub, so while in Miami, Mirm and Besse took her to hear a singer named Charlie Farrel. Every once in a while, as he sang his songs to an obviously overwhelming Jewish crowd, he would throw in a

---

*Note: The *mohel* at the *Brit Milah* for Leonard White, the author's husband, was Asa Yolson. This is Len's major claim to fame.

Yiddish word. To her dying day, Ma would never believe that Charlie Farrel was, in fact, not Jewish.

One winter, when Dolly was visiting from London, she took Ma to Bermuda instead of Miami Beach. Ma hated Bermuda and wanted to go back to Miami Beach. Dolly would not agree to this. Ma was disappointed, so she called her son-in-law, Dr. Sam Becker, and had him convince Dolly that it was much too cold for Ma in Washington, D.C. and they should both spend the winter in Florida. Dr. Sam took wonderful care of Ma and he was always her favorite Silverstone.

Chapter 3
DOLLY

Dolly, the oldest child, was the first to marry. Strong and independent, she was wed to a very wealthy man, Conrad Silverman, and had two sons, Mortimer and Mayer. They lived in London in a large, elegant home and were cared for by a household staff. Living in proper fashion was

Conrad and Dolly Silverman

extremely important to Dolly. When she visited the United States, her brothers and sisters prepared for it as though the Queen of England was coming for a visit.

When in Washington, D.C., Dolly stayed at the Sheraton Park Hotel where my parents, Mirm and Dr. Sam, lived and where Dr. Sam had his medical office.

On one visit, I went with my parents to meet Dolly at the airport and drive her to the hotel. Great effort had been made to reserve the best suite of rooms for her stay. As we approached her suite, followed by an array of men carrying a vast amount of luggage, Dolly stopped in her tracks and announced that the suite reserved for her would not do. The

Rebitzen Rebecca Silverstone and Children - 1948
Seated (left to right): Anna, Besse, Miriam, Ma, Rose, Dolly
Standing (left to right): Ellis, Joe, Herbie, Philip, Harry

room number was two-seventy-four. As she was supersti-
tious, staying in a suite whose numbers added up to thirteen
was unacceptable. The hotel had no other suites available at
that time. Pandemonium reigned until other, more suitable
rooms, were made available for Dolly's stay.

Dolly made it known that she was used to having her
bed turned down each night, but the hotel did not offer that
service. So, every night, Dolly was taken out for dinner. After
dinner, before returning her to the room, Dr. Sam would
drop Mirm off at the hotel on the pretense of checking his
office for calls. This delayed Dolly's return to her room, so
that Mirm would secretly have time to dash up to Dolly's
suite, turn down her covers, and lay her nightgown gently
on the bed. Each morning, Dolly would generously tip the
hotel maid for taking such good care of her. Mirm is still
waiting for *her* tip.

It was during one of Dolly's visits that the Silverstone
clan gathered at my house for an evening of conversation,
coffee, and desserts. Suddenly, Dolly noticed that her magnificent diamond bracelet was missing. A frantic search began and I, about eight years old at that time, joined in. I
had no idea what I was looking for as I began checking
behind sofa cushions and pillows. Suddenly, I felt a metallic
object and pulled up a string of colorful, sparkling stones.
Holding it up for all to see, I calmly asked, "Is this it?" And
it, it was. To this day I am still teased by my cousins with
the question calmly asked: "Is this it?"

When Dolly's son Mortimer was a young boy, he visited the United States with his brother, Mayer. Their Uncle
Phil took them for a ride in the country. Before driving them

back home, Phil required the two English boys to say, "America is better than England," and would not allow them back into the car until they did so. The two young British

Dolly's gift of jewelry gold, ruby and diamond pendant, pin and ring.

boys refused and walked miles and miles before they gave in, and finally said, "America is better than England."

During World War II, Mortimer was in the British Army stationed in Egypt. He was assigned to the staff of Anthony Eden. When Mortimer was able to get a few days off, he would request a staff car and drive to Palestine to see Ma and Da. The first time he went it was a Friday afternoon and, as he drove down their street, he realized that he did not know exactly where they lived. Mortimer stopped to ask for directions but after seeing that he was a British officer, no one wanted to help him.

"But I am the Rabbi's grandson," Mortimer said.

"Ahh, you mean Rabbi and Rebitzen Silverstone? Oh, then it is okay to give you directions," was the reply. "They live down this street."

Whenever Mortimer had leave, he would drive from Egypt to Palestine to spend the *Shabbat* with Ma and Da. Mortimer said that was the only time during the war that he would get a good meal.

During Dolly's last visit to Washington, D.C. in 1948, the Silverstone family, composed of Ma, five girls, and five boys, was able to come together for a family picture.

On the trip to the airport after this same visit, Dolly quietly slipped off the jewelry she was wearing and gave it to my mother and me for taking such good care of her.

Chapter 4
ANNA

A ll of the Silverstone sisters and brothers were in awe of Anna the next oldest child. Anna married Nathan Hurwitz, an expert olive oil taster, and lived in Marseille, France.

Nathan and Anna Hurwitz - Wedding Photo

They lived in a mansion and shared a lavish lifestyle. Unfortunately, their estate was next to a German munitions park that was bombed by an American aircraft during World War II. Their home was destroyed.

Nathan Hurwitz's younger sister Helene (Yitzak Gal's mother) and Anna Silverstone Hurwitz in front of Marseilles Estate. 1937.

The Hurwitz family was able to pack and store some of their china, linens, and antiques in an Italian Bank vault, and retrieved them after the war. Anna left France with her son and daughter, Myron and Doreen, and moved to Washington, D.C., while Nathan remained in Europe during the war. At age 15, son Myron published his one and only Volume 1 - No. 1 Silverstone Gossip News Letter.

Portions of Myron's Silverstone News:

A Gazette for the Propagation of Gossip
Vol. 1- No. 1   Friday March 22nd, 1940

Editorial: We have created this bulletin to propagate gossip among members of the Silverstone family. For this news bulletin we hope to start feuds between members of the family. When everyone is good and mad with everyone, then we will have reached our goal.

Synagogue news: Though the editors were not present, we have been told that last Friday Rabbi Harry delivered a fine speech on "Is there a Heaven and is there Hell?" Some members of the congregation, whom we will not name, got up and objected to such a speech in shul. The Rabbi held his place and the people shut up like a clam (tho' a clam is not kosher). Congratulations, Reverend.

Society: Last Sat. eve the gang met for the weekly poker game at Dr. and Mrs. Becker's residence. They served swell eats and the gang refused to leave before 3AM Mrs. Becker is the former Miriam Silverstone.

Work Info: Elinore Shrager got a job at the Emerald-toe Shop at 12th and G. Streets, N.W. Please try and buy your hose there so Elinore can keep her job.

Rosalie Silverstone secured a job in Lansburgh's French Millinery Dept. Congratulations.

Myron married an artist named Claudine. They moved to New York with their four children. Myron had a very successful career as a senior management executive with The Port Authority of New York and New Jersey's Interstate Transportation Department.

In 1987, Myron Hurwitz was awarded France's Legion of Honor by the French Ambassador to the United States.

Now retired, Myron and Claudine live in a restored farmhouse in Boussac, France. They travel to the United States several times a year to visit their children and grandchildren.

Myron's sister, Doreen, married a wealthy builder named Donald Brown. They had three children and lived in two magnificent homes, one in downtown Washington, D.C., and a country home in Maryland. Although very wealthy, every time Donald visited his mother-in-law, Anna, he would surreptitiously help himself to a small antique and slip it into his pocket as he left her home. Anna loved Don's cunning way of teasing her and would say, "I see what you're doing, Don." Don would feign innocence.

Anna retained her status as a connoisseur of style and grace. Whatever Anna said or did was "the law." Whenever a final decision had to be made about whether something was proper or not, we would hear, "Anna says...", and that was that.

Over the years, Anna acquired an exceptional collection

Collection of Rare Fans Shown

MRS. NATHAN HURWITZ (right) exhibited her collection of rare fans Saturday at the annual luncheon of the State Officers Club of the DAR. Mrs. John Morrison Kerr, president of the D.C. State Officers Club, is shown here assisting Mrs. Hurwitz.

Exhibiting her fan collection Washington, D.C., June 3, 1946.

Reclining Lady Statuette

of antique fans. These fans were displayed at many embassies and estates as fund raisers for various charities. Anna Hurwitz was considered a true celebrity in the Silverstone family.

Anna had a very beautiful Spanish shawl which she gave to Ma when Ma came to visit her in Marseilles. When Ma returned to America, she gave the shawl to Besse, who displayed it on her piano. Then, when Anna came to America and Besse needed a gift to give to *her,* Besse wrapped the same lovely shawl and passed it off to Anna as a new and special gift.

This re-gifting happened again with a pair of initialed earrings. Ma took these beautiful earrings from Anna to give as a gift to sister, Besse. Besse said the earrings were uncomfortable and gave them as a present to her younger sis-

Anna Silverstone Hurwitz

ter, Mirm. Mirm didn't care for earrings, so when Anna came to America, Mirm had the earrings gift-wrapped to give her as a present.

The best present of all, once when Da visited Anna in France, he admired a china figurine of a lady reclining with a book. Anna gave this figurine to Da to give to my mother, Mirm. When Da arrived home, he announced to everyone that he had traveled across the ocean with a "lady in his stateroom."

This was a very daring statement from the Vice President of the Union of Orthodox Rabbis of America! He then presented my mother, Mirm, with this beautiful porcelain statue of a lady. This figurine now lives with me and all are invited to visit and see her.

Anna had a custom of telling a story in conjunction with any gift she gave—and if she started to embellish a gift with a long explanation, we would call it an "Anna story." But everyone looked up to Anna as the criterion for good taste and manners.

Chapter 5
RABBI HARRY

Harry, gentle and scholarly, was the oldest son, and the only son to become a rabbi. He married Gertrude Greene from Buffalo, New York and, as a couple, they focused on Jewish life and charity. At their wedding, Gertrude met the whole Silverstone family for the first time and was confused when introduced to Bobsy. *Hmm,* she thought, *that would make 11 children and Harry said there were only 10.* Harry had neglected to tell her that Bobsy was a nickname for Ellis, and there really were only ten Silverstone children.

Young Rabbi Harry

Gentle and well educated, Harry had vast knowledge of the Talmud. He was also a wonderful storyteller. In his religious life, whenever

anyone asked Rabbi Harry a question, he or she rarely got
a specific answer. Instead, Rabbi Harry would relate a story
from the Torah or other religious teachings that would illus-
trate a moral answer.

But not so moral was the mistake Harry made when he
first met Gertrude, his future bride of sixty-plus years. Wanting to pay her a compliment, but getting his words a little
mixed up, Harry admired the pretty "beret" she was wearing
and said to Gertrude, "I really like that *bra* you are wearing
tonight." This comment was considered very risqué in the
1920's and the story was retold for years.

Rabbi Harry was a scholar, not a 'sophisticate', nor
worldly in social etiquette. At one of the first family recep-
tions he attended as a guest of his wife, Gertrude, he re-
marked how delicious the lamb chops were.

"What did you do with little paper sleeves that adorn
the lamb chop bones?" Gertrude asked, perplexed. Embarrassed, Harry had to sheepishly admit that he didn't know
they were for decoration and he had eaten them.

Rabbi Harry never gave direct answers to questions but
would tell stories and leave it to the listener to grasp the
righteous conclusion. One such story, which the children
loved to hear, was of a young rabbinical university student
who traveled to another city to begin his studies. The boy
was concerned about finances but his mother assured him
that if he studied the Bible every day, "God would provide."
(Da often made this same comment in response to the ever-
present question, "How will we manage with such a large
family?"). The young student was too busy with his studies
to bother reading the Bible, and would often call his mother

to express his panic at running out of money. His mother always offered the same response: "Study your Bible and God will provide." Finally, unable to continue his academic studies, the young student packed up his belongings and went home. There, he confronted his mother with the fact that God had not provided, and thus, he had run out of money. To which his mother responded, as she picked up his Bible and flipped through the pages,

"Had you studied your Bible as directed, you would have found, tucked into various pages throughout the book, ten, twenty, and fifty-dollar bills to finance you while you were away at school."

Another story Rabbi Harry shared concerned Shlomo the Poor, a solitary man who, although he went to synagogue everyday, lived alone and had few friends. When approached to give money for *tzedakah*, he would respond with a nod, turn, and walk away. He lived in a town where his neighbors appeared comfortable and didn't need his charity. Years passed and the requests to be charitable were always ignored. Then one day, many years later, Shlomo the Poor died. Suddenly the farmers had no food for their livestock, the children were wanting for school supplies, and the hospitals were in need of medicines. It did not take long for the town's people to realize that with the death of Shlomo came the death of many of the supplies that had been provided for them. The moral: The highest form of charity is to give anonymously.

This led us to inquire about the eight degrees of charity, each level greater than the next. The explanation was found in the Torah: Laws of Presents to the Poor. The Torah states that the highest form of giving is to help an indi-

vidual become self-sufficient, and therefore, no longer de-
pendent on another person or community. Next, is to give
anonymously. The giver does not know who the recipient is
and the recipient does not know their benefactor.

The next level of charity is when the donor knows to
whom he is giving, but the recipient does not know the
benefactor. Below that level is when the donor does not know
to whom he gives but the recipient does know his benefactor. The last four levels of charity, in order of worth, are to
give before being asked, to give after being asked, to give
willingly, and lastly, to give unwillingly. Of all the *mitzvot*
commanded in the Torah, taking care of a person in need is
the most important.

Rabbi Harry inherited the gift of storytelling mentioned
earlier from his father and told us the following tale. One
Sabbath, Harry was walking home with his father after the
morning service. That morning's Torah portion had been about
the coming of the *Messiah* and Harry asked how one would
know if the Messiah comes. In response, Da posed a question.

"Harry, today is Shabbat," he said, "a day when pious
Jewish people do not work or handle money. What would
you do if right now, if you should see a hundred dollar bill
laying on the sidewalk?"

Harry, knowing that it was the Sabbath, knew he could
not touch the money or pick-it up, so said he would kick it
with his foot until he got home.

"Ahh", said Da. "That would be considered work and is
not permitted on the Shabbat."

"Then I would step on it and stand here until sundown
when the Shabbat is over," said Harry.

*Gertrude and Harry
with Silverstone
family Torah*

"And miss the evening service?" asked Da. "That would not be acceptable."

"All right" replied Harry, "then what would *you* do if you saw a hundred dollar bill laying on the sidewalk on the Sabbath?"

Da replied, "Don't worry, when it happens, I'll know what to do."

In the early 1950's, Rabbi Harry retired as leader of the congregation, Tifereth Israel, the synagogue that his father had founded in 1914. The Silverstone family and friends would then meet for services and holidays in Rabbi Harry and Gertrude's home.

To honor Gedaliah's memory, we named that congregation Beth Gedaliah and everyone, family and friends alike, was welcome.

It was at one such service that I mentioned that I had

The 'Authentic'
Gedaliah Kiddush Cup

the one special *Kiddush* cup that had belonged to my grand-father, Rabbi Gedaliah. Several of my cousins challenged the veracity of my statement. Lo and behold, at the next service, three of my cousins showed up with the very same type of *Kiddush* cup, all claiming that theirs was the one and only authentic Rabbi Gedaliah *Kiddush* cup.

As a congregation, the Silverstones joined forces and purchased a torah that had been rescued in Czechoslovakia during the Holocaust. Virtually all synagogues located in what is now known as the Czech Republic were burned during World War II.

After another Friday night service, Harry's younger brother Phil was driving home with his son, Leslie, and commented that he thought Harry's sermon that night was exceptional. Leslie thought it was good, but was curious as to why Phil thought it was so special.

"It was short," was Phil's reply.

I can still hear the silence during one memorable High
Holiday service at Beth Gedaliah. In true orthodox tradition, only Jewish males who have become a *Bar Mitzvah* may
be called to read from the Torah for the honor of receiving
an *Aliyah*. At the conclusion of this service, Rabbi Harry
called each qualified male to the Torah in turn, according to
the hierarchy of their paternal heritage: first the Kohanim,
descendants of the Temple priests; next the Levites, descendants of the ancient tribe of Levi; and lastly, the Israelites,
the common people. As always, Rabbi Harry would ask, "Did
I forget anyone?"

Suddenly, completely breaking from tradition, cousin
Sherry, a young female in her twenties, began to approach
the Torah. Jaws dropped. Silence reigned. Aunt Gertrude, the
Rabbi's wife, to whom tradition was all important, ordered,

*Silverstone
Family Torah*

*Sherry Silverstone Holt
singing at family services*

"Sherry, sit down."

Sherry continued her quest, aiming to modernize our family services. She continued her walk to the Torah. Everyone froze. "Sherry, sit down" echoed throughout the room. In a very uncomfortable atmosphere, Sherry stopped, looked into Rabbi Harry's eyes and relented. Understanding the non-negotiable gaze confronting her, Sherry returned to her seat.

After the service, a discussion was held regarding tradition versus modernization. Although Rabbi Harry was willing to bend tradition in many ways, such as having the men and women sit together, a female receiving an *Aliyah* was going too far. It was not allowed. Yet Rabbi Harry continued to call Sherry, with her beautiful voice, to join him in the front of the room, and lead our congregation in singing the prayers. But allowing a woman to receive an *Aliyah* was beyond the reach of the Silverstone religious customs.

Yom Kippur, the day of Atonement, is the holiest day of the Jewish year. This is a day of fast and should be devoted to prayer and repentance, *nothing else*. Once, the females of the congregation had retired to the upstairs living room while the men completed the long day of praying. My mother Mirm, who was not usually outrageous, asked Rebitzen Gertrude if she and the Rabbi had ever had sex on *Yom Kippur*. Without missing a beat, Rebitzen Gertrude replied, "We can miss one night in the year."

Being the only Silverstone sibling to have no children, Rabbi Harry was a true scholar. Along with being an ordained rabbi, he had an active law practice for many years. Later in life, Harry studied and earned a Doctorate of Judicial Science (S.Jd.) from Georgetown University, the school run by Jesuit priests in Washington, D.C. The thesis for his dissertation was that the concepts underlying today's Anglo-Saxon law can be found in the ancient writings of the Torah Scrolls.

When it came time to defend his dissertation, *Modern Day Law and Religion*, he was asked by one of the professors if he would like to defend in English or in Hebrew. Being the true scholar that he was, his response to his dissertation committee was that he would like to defend in Aramaic, the language of the people at the time the Torah Scrolls were written. The committee then voted to have him defend in English.

One trait many Silverstones share is the "sleep-late gene." Nothing of importance ever happens before noon, and Rabbi Harry was no exception. After graduating from

Georgetown University at the top of his class, Rabbi Harry was invited to teach a course in Religion and the Law. The only problem was that the class was held at ten-thirty in the morning, which meant that Harry would have to wake as early as 8AM in order to dress, eat and arrive at the University in time. So he brought his dilemma up for discussion after one of our Friday night services. Rabbi Harry, at this time, was about seventy-five years young, and the consensus was that he had worked long and hard enough and it was time for him to sleep late and avoid additional stress. So he turned down the offer to teach.

The "sleep-late gene" appears again in the story about cousin Dr. Dan Silverstone, the son of cousin Dr. Leslie Silverstone of Boston, Massachusetts. While Dan was doing a two month clerkship for radiologists at the Armed Forces Institute of Pathology at Walter Reed Hospital, he was fortunate to be the houseguest of his uncle, Rabbi Harry, and Aunt Gertrude, who lived near the hospital.

Rabbi Harry, as always, was accustomed to sleeping very late each morning. So he told Dan to help himself to breakfast and leave quietly. Unknown to Dan, Rabbi Harry had his home wired with an alarm system. The very first morning of his visit, Dan had to be at the hospital by 6AM. He awoke and, as quietly as possible, got ready to go to the hospital. He crept down the stairs and gently opened the front door, not knowing that an alarm had been set to go off. And off it went, making a loud, wailing siren noise. Rabbi Harry, always so gentle, appeared at the top of the steps; his hair was tousled and he was in his pajamas. Dan was horrified and apologized emphatically.

"Don't worry," said Harry with a smile, "at least now we know the alarm works."

My mother Mirm's sleep-late rule was absolute. No one could wake her before noon. If the house was on fire, we were instructed to wait until the fire engines arrived, the ladders were in place against our house, and the firemen were climbing through her bedroom window. Then, waking her was permissible.

During Dr. Dan's stay in Washington, D.C., there was a huge snowstorm. Everything came to a halt, except for the Orthodox Jewish men who wanted to pray every morning. To conduct this early prayer service, called *shacharit*, there must be a *minyan*; ten Jewish men required for public worship. Because of the snowstorm, the men who usually participated in this service were not able to get to the temple.

A man from the temple knocked on Rabbi Harry's door and explained the predicament. Two more men were needed to make a *minyan*. And Rabbi Harry was one of them. So Dan, knowing that he must comply, and not able to dig his car out of the deep snow, put his uncle, a small man, on his back, and carried him through the snow to the Tifereth Israel Synagogue one block away. Of course, after the service, there was the same proposition. Dan had to carry Rabbi Harry back to his home. What a sight this must have been!

Rabbi Harry was well-known and well-liked. When I was growing up, the parents of most of my Jewish friends would tell me that my uncle had officiated at their marriage

ceremony. More precisely, they would say, in incorrect ver-
nacular, that my uncle "had married them."

One day, Gertrude was driving her car a bit too fast on
the way to purchase a *challah* for their Shabbat dinner. She
was stopped by a policeman who asked to see her driver's
license. When he saw that her name was Silverstone he asked
if she was related to the Rabbi.

"Yes," said Gertrude. "I am the Rabbi's wife."

The officer then said, "Oh, I'm your relative. My last
name is Silverstone, too."

Most important, he did not give Gertrude a ticket. She
then invited him to her home for dinner but the policeman
declined and was not heard from again.

The Silverstones loved to gamble. In his later years, as
a retired Rabbi in his eighties, Harry was a frequent visitor
to Atlantic City, New Jersey. He always came away a winner,
and when asked about the secret of his success, he would
allude that perhaps his lifetime of prayer had given him "di-
vine markers."

When Harry was a young man he looked out for his
younger brother, Ellis. After dating a young woman named
Lena Bishnow, Harry realized that he was not ready for marriage. He told Lena, "You should meet my brother, Ellis."

The introduction was made and, soon afterward, Ellis
and Lena were married.

Chapter 6
ELLIS

Ellis was the renegade of the family. As teenagers, Harry and Ellis were sent to Palestine to study at the *Yeshiva*. Because Harry was the older of the two boys, he was sent money every month to cover their expenses. One day, Ellis insisted that he wanted his share of the money in order to take care of things by himself. After much haggling, Harry reluctantly gave Ellis his share. Later that day, Ellis sheepishly returned and told Harry that he had lost his money. To this day, no one really knows what actually happened, but Harry and Ellis shared a spartan existence for that month.

Ellis and Lena's daughter, Rosalie, is a wonderful story teller with a delightful sense of humor. She recalls the many times Ellis would relate stories about Lena, who was sweet but not very worldly. Lena was originally from Russia and her English was a bit unique. Ellis loved to tell stories that were known as "Lena Stories." One such tale is about the time a large crowd was expected for dinner at the *Old Brick Inn* tavern they owned in Upper Marlboro, Maryland. Ellis told Lena to, "take all the steaks out of the freezer and thaw them out."

Lena did just that. Later, when the cook wanted to prepare the steaks, Ellis asked Lena where they were.

Lena and Ellis Silverstone, 1929.

"I did what you said," she replied. "I took out the steaks and threw them out."

One time, Lena was at a family party and met a lady from her hometown of Baltimore, Maryland. When the lady inquired about a man in Lena's family who was no longer living, Lena explained, "Right now he's dead!"

That "right now dead" expression is still used among the Silverstones.

On a trip to the horse races, a passion for most Silverstones, Ellis was driving Miriam, Sam, and some other friends. Everyone got into their cars and drove the short distance to the track. About one hour after they arrived, someone missed Lena and asked where she was.

"Hmm," responded Ellis, "I guess I forgot Lena and left her at home."

Needless to say, Lena was furious when everyone returned home later that afternoon saying, "I can see how you can forget your hat or your scarf, but how can you forget your wife?"

Lena tended to be absent-minded. On the morning of her only grandson's *Bar Mitzvah* service, she awoke with a headache. Reaching into the medicine cabinet, she quickly swallowed a couple of pills which she thought to be headache remedies. Taking a closer look, she discovered she had swallowed two sleeping pills. Poor Lena had a terrible time that day, trying to enjoy the festivities while struggling to stay awake.

Lena's husband, Ellis, was a master of the outrageous. Ellis wanted money to go to the races, "for a sure thing." He borrowed some money from the grocer next door and promised to pay

Lena Bishnow Silverstone

him back in a few days. When he lost the money, he borrowed more money from the owner of the liquor store two doors down for another, "sure thing." When it came time to pay up, he brought both store owners together and said, "You both are owed money so work it out between the two of you."

Another time, Ellis drove over to see younger brother Phil at his place of business, *Motor Credit Company*. Ellis double-parked his car, left the motor running with his keys in the ignition, and ran inside to say hi to Phil.

"Hey, let's go to the track," said Phil. So off they went, leaving Ellis's car double-parked, motor running, keys in the ignition, on a busy street in the business section of Washington, D.C. Who knows? The car may still be there.

And then there were the nightly poker games. As previously noted, Silverstones loved to gamble. This particular night, Ellis included Lena as a player around the poker table. As the evening progressed, Ellis noticed that Lena stayed in for every hand, losing more often than winning. Exasperated, Ellis finally asked Lena why she played every hand when she did not have good cards.

"You could sit out a hand or two," Ellis advised.

"No," replied Lena, "I didn't come here to relax."

The poker games ran very, very late. This particular night, the game was at brother Joe's house. It was way past midnight and Mirm said she smelled something burning. Rosalie, Lena's daughter, said she was so tired she didn't care if the house was burning down, she was not going to move. All of a sudden, Rosalie jumped up, realizing that, having dropped her cigarette, it was *she*, Rosalie, who was on fire.

At an all-night poker game at Rosalie's house, dawn was approaching and Rosalie's children, Robin and Gary, stumbled out of their bedrooms rubbing the sleep out of their eyes.

"What kind of mother are you?" asked Besse, "to let your children stay up all night?"

"What do you mean, stay up all night?" replied Rosalie. "The children are waking up to go to Sunday school!"

The Silverstone 'gene' for fun and humor has been passed on from generation to generation. An example of this is relayed by Rosalie's daughter, Robin, who at the time was in her thirties and still single. It was during a Christmas holiday time that Rosalie and Robin went shopping. The department store was very crowded, and Robin offered to stand in the cashier's line while her mother looked for some taupe-colored gloves. After searching for the gloves, Rosalie held up several pairs and called to Robin above the holiday crowd, "Are these taupe? How about this pair? Or this pair?"

Robin, embarrassed by the commotion her mother was causing, yelled back her response.

"Purple, beige, taupe ...I don't know, mother. What do you want from me?"

To which Rosalie screamed, for all the shoppers to hear, "I want that you should get married!!" Several months later Robin became Mrs. Ken Loren.

The Silverstones were very social. They loved to talk and gossip. One night, Miriam and Rosalie were driven to the Washington, D.C. airport to catch a flight to Plainfield, New Jersey to visit with their sister, Besse. They sat in the airport lounge waiting for the plane's departure and began to talk. And talk and talk they did. After a while, it seemed like they had waited a long time, and went to check on the plane's departure time. The attendant told them that the plane had left on-time thirty minutes ago, and that their names had been announced over the airport's loud speaker several times. Mirm and Rosalie were so busy talking that they never heard the departure announcements and missed their flight to New Jersey. They then proceeded to take a cab to Union Station and caught a train to New Jersey.

Chapter 7
BESSE

The stories about Besse, the third oldest daughter, run the gamut from the very naive but determined girl in Washington, D.C., to Herman's supposedly helpless wife in New Jersey, to an independent, stubborn and self-reliant woman.

One given was that Besse had the most beautiful complexion of all the Silverstone women. Her explanation was that, with ten children in the house, she never had the luxury of washing the soap off her face, and that was the secret of her beautiful skin.

As an older teen, Besse had the clever idea that cigarettes, which were in style at that time, could be sold from vending machines in places like gasoline stations and street corners so that smokers wouldn't have to enter a store to make a purchase. Every-

Besse and Herman

one discouraged this idea, saying that it would make cigarettes too available for young children. Future trends proved
everyone wrong, and Besse never profited from her idea.

Besse was very popular and once had a date with Mor-
ris Cafritz, a future millionaire, but he started talking marriage on the first date. This scared Besse so much that she
jumped out of his car and walked home. That was the end
of her chance to be *rich*.

Ma and Da did not want Besse to marry a soldier named
Herman Shrager, whom she met at a dance for servicemen
during World War I. Herman was stationed in Washington,
D.C. and it was love at first dance. During their courtship,
Besse would correspond daily with Herman. Not wanting
her mother to know about this, Besse would pay her youngest sister, Mirm, five cents to walk down to the mailbox and
mail the letter. Ever the entrepreneur, young Mirm would
take the daily letters entrusted to her and sell them to their
mother for ten cents. Luckily, in the end, true love prevailed,
and Besse and Herman were married.

In an attempt to discourage the romance, Ma sent Besse
to Marseilles, France to spend time with her sister, Anna.
However, Besse returned home, and she and Herman managed to elope in Baltimore, where they were married by Rabbi
Leventhal. Herman was worried about his mother's reaction
to his getting married without her being there, so they kept
the elopement a secret from his family, and Ma and Da arranged a 'wedding' in a New York hotel, just so Herman's
mother could attend.

The day of the wedding, Herman's mother decided not
to go, so all the expense was for nothing - except that a

few important 'Plainfielders' did come. This date was June 9, 1920, and their first child, Elinore, was not born until July, 1922, so anybody who thought they *had* to elope, was wrong.

Herman became a CPA, and two more children, Marvin and Robin, completed their family.

Besse knew absolutely nothing about keeping house or cooking meals, and it was a standing joke that when her brothers came to Plainfield they were served her specialty: tuna fish salad. Ma told Besse that she should never do any housework so there was always a housekeeper to take care of the home. Her husband, Herman, however, loved to go shopping, and made sure there was always a full ice-box, with plenty of canned tuna fish in the pantry in case Besse decided to cook.

Despite this 'handicap', Besse learned to become a wonderful hostess, and gave a big theme party every year — usually a costume party — that the elite of Plainfield, New Jersey Jewish society attended. Just before one of her large parties, Besse got a phone call telling her that the water in the city was being turned off and that she had better be prepared. So she ran around the house, filling every pitcher, pan and jar, as well as all the bathtubs. When the prankster, who was one of her guests, arrived, everyone had a good laugh!

Phil always told the story about coming to Plainfield, New Jersey when Besse had a gathering of friends for supper. Besse was afraid there might not be enough food, so she told Phil (and maybe Joe or Ellis, too) FHB (Stands for Family Hold Back). Phil said he was starving, but every time the platter of food came around, Besse would remind him about FHB, and he would say he wasn't hungry. Phil loved to tell that story for years and years.

During the Depression, Ellis' wife, Lena, and daughter, Rosalie, came to live with the Shrager family in Plainfield. Ellis had owned a grocery store in Philadelphia, and he brought all the canned goods he could carry, so Besse's storeroom was like a little grocery store. Ellis worked in a shoe store in Plainfield, and when he got paid, he would spend his whole salary buying toys for Besse and Herman's son, Marvin—much to Lena's dismay.

One day, Ellis decided to paint the Shrager's house to show his gratitude for their hospitality. He climbed up a tall ladder to get to the third floor where he planned to start the painting. Suddenly he felt someone behind him at the top of the ladder. It was Marvin, who was only about four years old. Somehow, Ellis managed to get Marvin, himself, and the can of paint safely down the ladder; it was a story that was told for years.

Eventually, Ellis moved his family back to Maryland and bought a tavern in Upper Marlboro called *The Old Brick Inn*. As children, we all loved to visit there because the tavern had gambling slot machines and lots of delicious, *traif* food. And Ellis always had a gleam in his eye as to what kind of mischief he could stir up next.

This particular day, my cousins Leslie and Stuart, young sons of Philip and Sadie, were visiting. These boys also had a gleam in their eyes. It was a slow, boring day at the tavern, so Ellis said he would give five dollars to the first boy to throw a baseball through a closed window. One of the boys did just that; glass went flying everywhere and excitement once again reigned at the tavern.

Besse was very active in organizations in Plainfield. She was one of the founders of the Plainfield Chapter of Hadassah, and the president for many years. She also proved to be a very successful fund-raiser and raised more money for Hadassah and for the Jewish Community Center than anyone else in town. One of her ideas was a child popularity contest, where parents and friends could buy votes by making donations. She raised a lot of money for the charity and also got her daughter, Robin, voted the most popular child in Plainfield.

Besse tried to educate her sisters-in-law, Jessie and Lena, in what is now referred to as Women's Lib, but in those days was, "Don't be a doormat." I doubt if her brothers, Joe and Ellis, appreciated Besse telling their wives to stand up for their rights, but Besse, clearly ahead of her time, didn't care.

Besse's daughter, cousin Elinore, remembers summers at Bradley Beach, NJ. There were always visitors sharing their modest beach house. Jessie and her children, Elaine and Elwood, would walk past a fish market in order to get to the beach. No one recalls who started the chant, "I SMELLLLLLL SOMETHING," but it was repeated for years.

Besse was widowed at the age of 51, assuming she was born in 1900, a date she decided on because her birth certificate was non-existent. It was easier to always be the age of the current year! Several years after her husband Herman died, Besse moved to Washington, D.C., into the Woodner Hotel, the one place she knew she could live without having to cook, as there was a coffee shop and a dining room in the hotel. She enjoyed her life there for 15 years, but the hotel went downhill, and after being robbed while she was asleep in her apartment, she was finally convinced to move to the Revitz House in Rockville, Maryland.

One night, my family was taking Besse and a neighbor out to dinner. The neighbor had been recently deserted by her husband and she was included in the invitation as a neighborly gesture. Always the tease, Dr. Sam told Besse to ask the woman why her husband left her. No sooner had the neighbor put her foot into our car then Besse said, "Sam wants to know why your husband left you."

We were all horribly embarrassed that Besse didn't realize Dr. Sam was kidding with her when he made his original suggestion to inquire about our neighbor's marital status.

Besse's deceased husband had a wealthy cousin named Max, who lived in South Africa. He met Besse and wanted to marry her. But he also wanted Besse to live with him in South Africa. Besse and her cousin, Marie Silverstone, actually made a trip to South Africa and were lavishly wined and dined by Max's family, friends, and relatives. But Max wasn't well, and Besse wasn't interested in moving to a foreign country. She came home without making a commitment. Nate, Besse's son-in-law, never forgave her for giving up the chance to be *rich* for the second time in her life!

Besse's son, Marvin, vividly recalls his consternation when Miriam and Sam Becker unexpectedly appeared at his wedding to Sara. Only immediate family was invited and Marvin and Sara were so nervous that other family members would find out. Now this incident is a source of fond memories of the uninvited, but most welcomed, guests.

A more dramatic incident occurred years later at a dinner party in Washington, D.C. Marvin and Sara were sitting quietly, talking and eating, when gentle, well-mannered Miriam suddenly started beating Sara frantically on her head with a cloth napkin. After the initial shock, everyone at the table realized that Sara's hair had caught on fire from an ill-placed candle. Only Miriam's quick action had averted a serious injury.

Chapter 8
ROSE

Next in line was sister Rose. She was quiet and gentle in comparison to the other Silverstones. My mother, who was much younger than Rose, told me that she would often find small, nicely-wrapped presents on her night table when she awoke in the morning. It wasn't until many years later that Mirm discovered that these wonderful presents that appeared so magically were from Rose.

Da wanted Rose to marry a young Rabbi he knew, but Rose was definitely not interested. So when she was introduced by a mutual friend to Nathan Shapiro, they married after only six weeks of courtship in July of 1923.

Rose and Nathan had three daughters.

Rose

Annette was born first in 1926, followed by Lenora in 1928, and finally Joan was born ten years after Annette in June 1936.

Unfortunately Rose and Nathan's marriage was not a happy one.

Rose died much too young, the first of the ten Silverstone children to pass away. At the time of her death, she was just fifty-nine.

Chapter 9
JOE

Next in line was brother Joe. He appeared tough, but had a heart of gold. When anyone had a problem they would go to Joe, and he was always willing to help them. Joe Silverstone met his wife, Jessie, in business school. They married and had two children, Elwood and Elaine. Silverstone men had their eyes out for a good-looking woman and Jessie, Joe's wife, was one of the real beauties of Washington, D.C. One day, Jessie and Joe went to the movies. When the movie was over, Joe said he had to go to the men's room and would meet Jessie in the lobby of the theatre.

While waiting for Joe, Jessie looked at the poster display of coming attractions. When Joe walked out of the men's room, he saw the back of a woman he thought was Jessie, went up behind her, and gave her a pinch on the *tush*.

"Let's go, Jessie," he said.

But the lady with the *tush* was not Jessie.

Joe wasn't pleased when his young son, Elwood, had an itch on his knee, got scissors, and proceeded to cut a hole in his pants so that he could scratch his knee more easily.

When Elaine and Elwood were young, their Aunt Anna brought her children, Myron and Doreen, to visit their cousins who lived above their father Joe's car store, *Reliable*

Motors. As usual, Myron and Doreen were dressed in the finest clothes. They stayed with their cousins for an afternoon of polite playing. Elwood and Elaine were dressed as one would expect children living above a car store in a commercial Washington, D.C. area would be. Much to her dismay, when Anna returned to get her children, she found everyone out on the Fourteen Street 'street-car tracks' playing a rough-and-tumble game of football.

Jessie and Joe's family had a favorite candy called *Valati's.* They loved to sit around and talk about all the cavities they would get and all the weight they would gain as they devoured those chewy, sticky, gooey, wonderful caramels. Their son Elwood grew up and became a dentist. Maybe their love

of *Valati's* led him to that profession. To this day, *Valati's* candies can still be purchased at the Hecht Company Stores in the Washington metropolitan area.

But on this particular day, Joe and Jessie drove their children, Elwood and Elaine, to the candy store. The parents waited in the car while their children went into the

Jessie and Joe Silverstone
Washington, D.C.
around 1940 in front of their
house on Somerset Street N.W.

store to make the purchase. Walking back to the car, they each held one side of the bag full of candy, fighting over who would hold the bag. Each child pulled, tugged, argued and struggled until the bag ripped in half and all the candy fell into the street and down the gutter. That was the end of Valati's for that day.

The sweet-tooth gene must have been passed on to Elwood's sister Elaine and her grandson Jason. When Jason was seven years old and visiting his grandparents in Florida, they decided to have an 'all dessert dinner'. The deal was that for one night they would frequent three different restaurants and have one dessert dish for an appetizer, one dessert for the entrée and then, of course, a dessert for dessert. Jason and grandfather Irv had a grand time but poor Elaine spent the remainder of the night praying that she would live through the night.

As adults, Elaine and Elwood each married and continued to live in the Washington, D.C. area where they reared their children and maintained their family connections.

Chapter 10
HERBIE

Eighth in line was brother Herbie. He loved to joke but was not as outgoing as his older brothers. He also did not take his responsibilities seriously, but found ways to be mischievous so as not to get lost in the shuffle. In his teenage years, it was Herbie's job to deliver an *etrog* (a lemon-like fruit) and *luluf* (a type of fern leaf) to the religious congregants for the *Sukkot* holiday. One time, Herbie forgot to collect the money for these items. So when he returned home, Da reprimanded him and told him to write to all the recipients and bill them for the *etrog* and *luluf*. Herbie wrote letters to all the people saying, "Please Remit Money for the *etrog* and *luluf* that I brought to you for last *Pesach* holiday."

Da was most embarrassed by Herbie's lack of knowledge concerning the various Jewish holidays.

During World War II, Herbie was a warrant officer. After the war, he traveled with Ma to Marseilles to visit Anna. Back home in Washington, D.C., he went to work for the U.S. Post Office. Herbie also kept busy selling razor blades and pens on the side, and would generously give them free of charge to all the relatives who would take them. Herbie and his wife, Rae, had two sons, Kenny and Steven. They

*Herbie
with Ma
Silverstone
- circa
1950
Washing-
ton, D.C.*

attended all of the Silverstone family gatherings but were
not as social as their Silverstone relatives. Both sons married. Steven had two children, but neither of Herbie's sons
stayed connected with the Silverstone family.

Chapter 11
PHIL

Philip (Phil), the last son born, always had a trick up his sleeve. As teenagers, Phil and Joe wanted to make some money. They made a chicken coop and raised chickens to get eggs to sell. The chickens would not cooperate, so Phil and Joe took some eggs from Ma's icebox and sold them to Ma—over and over again.

Phil was sent to New York for the *Yeshiva,* the Rabbinical school, and called home the next day with the news that he was coming home because the school did not have a football team. And home he came.

Ma and Da were very hospitable, and often had relatives staying with them. Brothers Phil and Joe did not like a young English cousin named Annie who was a guest in their home. So one night, when Annie was coming home late from a movie, she walked into the darkened vestibule. As she proceeded up the steps very quietly, so as not to disturb anyone, she stepped into pans of water that Phil and Joe had strategically placed on each step.

Phil married a young woman named Sadie Stone and they had two sons, Leslie and Stuart. They lived on 16th Street N.W. Washington, D.C., near many other Silverstone homes.

Sadie and Phil with sons Stuart and Leslie,
On the Boardwalk in Atlantic City, NJ Circa 1947

One winter, Phil was driving his family to Miami Beach, Florida for a vacation. The boys, sitting in the backseat, started a pillow fight. The next thing Phil knew, he was driving 60 miles an hour down a highway and could not see a thing. Feathers from the busted pillows had filled the car and were flying everywhere. Phil could barely bring the car to a safe stop; he was furious.

Phil had to collect money owed to him. He asked Ellis to drive him to the man who owed the money. When they arrived at their destination, they saw that the man's house was surrounded by a big fence restraining about '101 ferocious looking dogs' (a Silverstone exaggeration). Phil was not about to approach the man's house. But Ellis opened the gate, walked forcefully past the '101 dogs' and knocked on the door. When the man opened the door, he was so shocked to see that someone had walked past his dogs that he gave Ellis the money owed to Phil.

Phil was to be the last, or ninth, Silverstone child. He was affectionately nicknamed 'Babe.' But several years later, my mother made her appearance.

Chapter 12
MIRIAM

Mirm was born in 1912 in the family home at 410 K Street N.W., in Washington, D.C. The address is important because in her later, gambling years, Mirm surreptitiously used the services of a 'bookie' to place her bets on the number '410', much to my father's chagrin. Mirm was the beauty of the family and my father, Dr. Sam, was her beau and husband for 55 years. He treated her like a princess. Although teased by his friends, Sam served Mirm breakfast in bed every morning for the 55 years they were together.

When younger sister Mirm was about ten years old, Philip was told to go to pick up some live chickens for the holiday on which you *shlogen kapores* which means that a prayer is said while swinging a live chicken above your head. (Yes, I know this sounds very strange, but that is the Orthodox custom.) Philip insisted that Mirm go along for the streetcar ride. On the way home, the chickens got loose from their ties. Phil jumped off the streetcar and left little Mirm alone to deal with all of the live chickens running wildly around.

Philip wanted to be generous to Mirm, whom he referred to as Angel, and he would use gambling as a way of giving her small amounts of money. On several occasions, when they were together at a wedding or other social event, Phil would casually say to Mirm, "I'll bet you five dollars that the next person who walks through that door is a blonde woman (or a fat man, etc.)."

Phil always paid his debt when his guess was wrong, and Mirm never turned down the money. I don't remember my mother ever paying her debt if she was wrong, but no one kept score.

When Mirm was a teenager, Ma would mysteriously place dollar bills in her purse when she wasn't looking. Mirm was oblivious to her financial status, and it was years later that Ma told her what she had done. After Ma told Mirm her secret, my mother relayed the story to me, and I started putting dollar bills in my oldest daughter, Jill's, wallet when she was occupied elsewhere. I still do this today and my daughter hasn't seemed to notice. Or if she does, she hasn't said a word so that the money will continue to magically appear. I guess that secret is out now.

When Mirm was sixteen years old, Phil bought her a used Marmon—a very expensive car at that time. Mirm drove it for a year. When she was seventeen, she was driving to a luncheon given in her honor because she was leaving for London the following day. She was driving the car full of girlfriends when one of the passengers in the front seat accidentally dropped her cigarette on Mirm's foot, which was on the gas pedal. Mirm slammed her foot on the gas pedal and drove the car over a platform called a 'dummy policeman' and wrecked the car. Mirm then proceeded to the luncheon and called Phil to inform him that he should pick up the car at a certain location because she was leaving for Europe the next day.

The story of my parents' courtship is a saga to be told. My mother Mirm, always a bit of a rebel, was engaged to be married to a wealthy young man from Buffalo, New York. An elegant engagement party was held and Mirm received many expensive gifts. At this time, Mirm's sorority had a Sadie Hawkins night where a lady could invite a man as her date. One of Mirm's friends, Esther Cafritz Ornstein, came to the party with Dr. Samuel Becker. Not knowing it was a hay ride, both arrived in formal attire. This made quite a negative impression on Mirm. Several months later, Mirm was shopping in Lansburg's Department Store in Washington, D.C. when she fell and cut her leg. After being treated by her family's physician, she was told that in order to have the store pay the medical costs, she would have to be seen by the insurance company's consulting physician, Dr. Samuel M. Becker.

Remembering the hay ride fiasco, Mirm said there was no way she was going to his office. But, desperately needing the money, Dr. Sam said he would go to Mirm's house. They met there and he asked her to go for a ride. In the late 1920's, cars did not have heat. Dr. Sam opened the car door for her and wrapped a blanket over her lap. Mirm was impressed with how well he treated her and decided to break off her engagement to her Boston fiancé. The only question at hand was what to do with all the engagement presents. Rules of etiquette would require that the presents be returned. The Silverstones reasoned that, since most of the gifts had already been used in some fashion, they should remain in the Silverstone family as a reminder of Mirm's first engagement.

Mirm's brother, Herbie, had a dog named *Traif*. One Sunday morning, Mirm invited her fiancé, Dr. Sam, for breakfast after they had gone horseback riding. Mirm didn't realize that Herbie had given his dog all the coffee cream that she had bought for this special breakfast. There was no cream for the coffee. But Dr. Sam married Mirm anyway, and that was probably the last time Mirm ever prepared a meal for him.

The year was 1931 and my parents, Mirm and Sam, were about to marry. It was decided that it would be impossible to invite all the members of Da's congregation to this wedding, but it would also be impossible not to. The final solution was to move the wedding to Plainfield. Besse's husband, Herman Shrager, offered his Prescott Hill Country Club as the site. It was a beautiful affair.

Mirm Silverstone & Dr. Sam Becker on horseback-1931

Da did invite a dozen Orthodox rabbis from the neighboring cities to officiate at the wedding. The country club did not have a kosher kitchen, so Herman arranged for special kosher catering to be brought in. Not knowing about the *Kashruth* tradition and, as a special favor to Herman, the country club served hors d'oeuvre of shrimp, crabmeat and clams to all the guests. The Orthodox rabbis thought everything was delicious.

Mirm went to New Jersey a day early to get ready for their wedding in Plainfield. Dr. Sam, not wanting to leave his medical practice, drove to Plainfield the day of the wedding, and was fearful of being late. He started speeding and was pulled over by a policeman who, at seeing Sam's medical insignia on the car, sarcastically asked, "Doctor, are you rushing to deliver a baby?"

Dr. Sam replied honestly, "No, I'm rushing to get married. I'm going to be late for my own wedding."

The officer responded, "I'll let you off today without a ticket, but ten years from now you'll be sorry I didn't put you in jail!"

Many years later, Mirm and Sam reciprocated to Besse and Herman Shrager for making the arrangements for their wedding by hosting a wedding for their

Katubah for Miriam
Judith Silverstone and
Samuel Becker, MD, 1931

Becker Home and Office 16th Street NW, Washington, D.C.

daughter, Robin, and her fiancé, Eddie, in their home on 16th Street in Washington, D.C.

Miriam Judith Silverstone and Dr. Samuel M. Becker had two daughters, Marlene and Judy (that's me) and moved into a house on 16th Street, N.W. Eventually, Dr. Sam renovated the entire basement level of the house into his medical office, selling the pool table to make way for his X-Ray table.

My father, Dr. Sam, embraced Mirm's family as the family he never had. In turn, all of the Silverstones received free medical care. Because Dr. Sam's medical office was located in the basement of our house, one or more of the Silverstones were in his office nearly everyday. After being treated, my aunts, uncles, and cousins would come upstairs to visit in our home. My father loved it, and I grew up knowing a closely knit family.

Because Mirm, my mother and the baby of her family, was treated like a true princess, she chose not to learn to cook. Either a housekeeper or my father prepared all the edible meals. Occasionally, Mirm did light our gas oven and throw a steak or lamb chops onto the broiler. On one particular day, Mirm came home a little before 6PM from either a social afternoon of lunch and cards or a charity event. She needed to quickly start dinner. It was winter and cold and the ovens in those days were ignited by striking a match and lighting the gas burner, which she did efficiently. Only problem was that Mirm, cook par excellence, neglected to remove the full-length mink coat she was wearing. As she put her arm into the oven to light the pilot, the fur sleeve caught fire and went up in flames. When the Liberty Mutual insurance adjuster came to our house to write up the claim, he asked if she had been smoking.

"Oh, no," Mirm replied, "I was cooking!"

The insurance adjuster then asked if he could write that she was smoking because cooking in a full-length mink coat was a tad unusual.

"No," she said emphatically and with pride, "I was cooking!"

And thus the report was submitted.

When Mirm did cook, she had her own particular protocol: one course at a time. When my husband, Len, and I became engaged, he was invited for dinner. Peas were served; the Becker family ate. Len sat there, waiting for the remainder of the dinner. Then, baked potatoes made their appearance. The Becker family ate. Len sat there, waiting. Finally, Mirm said, "Len, eat your peas and potatoes; they're getting cold."

Len was perplexed. We, the Becker family, found nothing unusual in the manner in which dinner was presented. Finally, the timer rang, the steaks were ready, and dinner proceeded as usual. To this day, Len still teases me about, "dinner in segments at the Becker house."

Phil was good to his younger sister, Mirm, and made sure she didn't have to clean the kitchen either. Every night at six-thirty, when dinner was usually finished, Phil was sure to call to discuss the important issues of the day while Dr. Sam cleaned the kitchen. This was a ruse that went on for years. I now realize how unique the solution was in the way that my parents dealt with some bothersome neighbors who they referred to as 'The Drop-ins.' This very wealthy, older couple obviously had time on their hands. They did not have to stay home on weekends and clean their house or take care of their children. So every Sunday afternoon at about 3PM, they would take the one block stroll from their house to our house to visit, uninvited, with my parents. My parents, not wanting to be rude, would offer tea and some desserts. Weekly, my parents would be annoyed at the time spent entertaining people that they did not care for.

So my parents constructed a plan. They brought two suitcases stuffed with newspaper into our front hallway. The plan was that the next time the "Drop-ins" showed up at our front door, I was instructed to explain that my parents were getting ready to leave on a trip, and the very visible suitcases would back up my statements.

Lo and behold, the next Sunday at about 3PM, there was the familiar knock on our front door. I was only about seven or eight years old at the time. I opened the door properly as instructed and called to my parents that the 'Drop-ins' were here again to visit. Something clicked. It was either my announcement or the ready to travel suitcases, but the 'Drop-ins' never appeared at our front door again.

Mirm loved to learn and was the only Silverstone daughter to attend college. She played a mean game of poker, collected Master Bridge Points which she used as book markers, and gave endless hours to various charity pursuits.

One of her charity endeavors included providing craft sessions for the patients at St. Elizabeth's Institution in Washington, D.C. For many years, this was a government facility that housed mentally ill patients. The craft projects were sold and the money given to the individuals who made them. On this particular day, the session was over, the patients were escorted back to their rooms, and the volunteers working with Mirm packed up the supplies. They were ready to leave when they realized that the scissors still had to be gathered up and accounted for. Mirm offered to stay behind and take care of the scissor situation. So the other volunteers left, closing the door behind them—which automatically locked. When Mirm was ready to leave she went to the door and was unable to get out. So she pushed a table over to the door, put a chair on top of the table, climbed up as best she could, and called through the transom that she was a volunteer, not a patient, and needed to get out. Doctors walked past the door, nurses walked past the door, and everyone ignored Mirm's furtive pleas. This type of behavior was not unusual in a mental institution. It was starting to get dark outside and Mirm was sure that her husband, Dr. Sam, would realize that she was missing. But Dr. Sam was busy with his work and didn't notice that she was not at home. Mirm started to panic, and yelled more and more, but her pleas for help were ignored by all who passed by the door. Finally, around 9PM, Dr. Sam noticed that Mirm had not returned home. He called St. Elizabeth's Institution and a search party was sent to rescue her. Sam was vehement that Mirm not return to this type of volunteer work, but the next week, back she went.

The year was 1954 and segregation was still in affect. In a passive way, my mother Mirm supported social causes and social change. I was present during a luncheon in our home with her bridge-playing friends. Dessert was being served and Gladys, our wonderful, black housekeeper, was preparing coffee. One of the more demanding ladies, Mrs. S., ordered Gladys to bring her a cup of coffee. Gladys, a large, buxom woman, was adored by our extended Silverstone family and friends, and she took no nonsense from anyone. Gladys spun around at this demand. Facing Mrs. S, hands on her hips, Gladys responded in no uncertain terms, "If you want coffee, go into the kitchen and get it yourself."

Discussions concerning this incident dominated the afternoon and evening. Mirm stood by Gladys in her defense.

At a Seder in the early 1950's, many of the Silverstones living in the Washington area came again to Rabbi Harry's house to join the Passover festivities. For this special occasion my mother, Mirm, hired some people who worked at a catering company to help with the serving and massive clean-up afterwards. The Seder began, the Hebrew prayers and songs were simultaneously chanted by all fifty to sixty people, and the catering workers, unaccustomed to hearing such a thing, *panicked*. Yelling to their co-workers that we were Holy Rollers, they grabbed their belongings, ran out of the house, and were never heard from again. To this day, the Silverstones still laugh when they remember the catering people running for their lives to get away from the house of fanatics!

At the end of the evening, the Rebitzen was over-whelmed with literally hundreds of plates, glasses and silver-ware. So all of the women gathered as many dishes, etc. as they could, put them into laundry baskets, and took them to their individual homes to wash, dry, and deliver them back to the Rabbi's house the following day.

After Mirm's husband, Dr. Sam, died, her final twelve years were difficult. She lived alone, by choice, and was in much pain from various medical conditions. Mirm commented that she had lived a terrific seventy-six years. It was

Samuel and Miriam Becker, circa 1960. Washington, D.C.

a charmed life, surrounded by family and friends. She was eighty-eight years old when she died.

As a widow, Mirm could be difficult, but retained her wonderful sense of humor. One night, my husband, Len, and I made one of our many grocery deliveries. Mirm was having her bridge-card-playing friends over the next afternoon, and to make our life easier, we decided to take a small case of sodas to her apartment, in hopes of cutting down on our all-too-frequent deliveries. When Mirm saw that we had bought more than the six sodas she had requested, she was adamant that we return the extras to the store. Len tried to reason with her that she had plenty of storage space and would use the extra sodas for future guests.

"No," Mirm insisted. "If you don't take them back I'll throw them in the trash."

Len tried to explain how this would make it easier for us not to have to make daily trips to the store and asked her why. What was her logic in refusing to keep the extra sodas?

Without missing a beat, Mirm replied, "Because when I die I want to come out even!"

And so the sodas went to our house for storage.

About a year before she died, Mirm fell and had to be rushed to the hospital. As I was riding with her in the ambulance she said, "Tell Len when he gives my eulogy to *emphasize my charity work and lay low about my gambling.*"

At the hospital, the admitting physician asked my mother the usual questions, "What date is it? Who is the current President?" etc.

"If I had known there was going to be a quiz," she responded, "I would have studied."

Chapter 13
FAMILY CONNECTIONS

During his lifetime, Rabbi Gedaliah published 38 books, which are commentaries on the Jewish holidays, customs and interpretations of the Torah. A Passover *haggadah* has two purposes: one; to tell the history of the Jewish peoples' forced exodus from Egypt to Palestine under the order of the Pharaoh and two; to give the exact order to be followed during the Passover *Seder*. The word 'seder' means 'order', and there is a precise format for this service.

One of his books, a *Pesach Haggadah,* was published in 1911. Included in the dedication was his hope that all ten Silverstone children would join together to share the Passover *Seder*. For many years, when Rabbi Harry and his wife Rebitzen Gertrude were alive, the Washington, D.C. Silverstones would meet at their house for this traditional dinner. Now, with the extended Silverstone family so large and living in several different cities, Gedaliah's grandchildren share their *Seder* with their own nuclear families, which include Gedaliah's grandchildren, their spouses, great-grandchildren and great-great grandchildren.

In 1939, Rabbi Gedaliah revised the original 1911 Haggadah and published a second edition, dedicated to me,

Judith Leah, the Rabbi's most recent grandchild. The 1911 Haggadah presented the Passover service in one font, accompanying commentary in a different font and the 1939 contemporary commentary in a third font.

At one Seder in 1946, the Silverstone family was seated

Title page of 1939 Passover Haggadoh and dedication to his daughter Miriam, her husband Dr. Becker and the author Judith Leah.
* Note the misspelling of "darling"

DEDICATION

With my sincere blessings, I dedicated this הגדה של פסח to my darlig daughter Miriam, her husband, Dr. Samuel Becker; and their sweet daughter Judith Leah

FATHER

around the table when the telephone rang. Mirm got up to answer the phone, thinking it might be a call for her husband, Dr. Sam. The call was actually from the International American Red Cross and they were looking for someone with the last name of, 'Gurwitz'*. Without giving it much thought, Mirm said there was no one at this number with that name. She then returned to the Seder table and relayed the strange call.

"Wait," said my uncle Nathan Hurwitz, "Gurwitz" was my family name. It is the Russian form of the name Hurwitz".

The rest of the evening was spent trying, to no avail, to contact the Red Cross in Europe. It was later learned that a cousin of Nathan's named Yitzak Gal* had survived internment in a concentration camp and was hoping to locate his family in America. The connection was not made, and Yitzak was sent to settle in Palestine, now Israel, where he married and had three wonderful sons and several grandchildren. Yitzak worked for IBM, connected with his American relatives, and has remained in contact with the Silverstone family to this day.

---

*Yitzak Gal was released from the concentration camp by the British Army on May 3, 1945. At that time his name was Isaac Gelkin. His name was changed to Yitzak Gal in Israel. In an email dated 10-13-04, Yitzak explained that the name was originally Gurwitz because there is no "H" in Cyrillic languages.

Chapter 14
INTUITION AND SMALL WORLD COINCIDENCES

I still ruminate about what I could have done differently in my efforts to make a Silverstone-Gal family connection. In June 2000, while visiting in Israel, my husband and I hosted a dinner party for the two families and some friends. Although they lived within a 20 minute drive of each other, the Israeli Silverstone families and the Gal families were not aware of each other and the familial connection. Yitzak Gal's uncle, Nathan Hurwitz, had married my aunt Anna Silverstone. Our dinner party was held on the rooftop restaurant, Abu Lafia, which overlooks the city of Tel Aviv. It was a magical evening, but the Silverstones socialized among themselves at one end of the long table and the Gals congregated at the other end.

I did plan ahead and had placemats showing the family tree connections. The food was plentiful and the conversations lively and no one looked at the placemats. It never occurred to me to have place cards so that the guests would be forced to mingle, or to have everyone introduce themselves.

Yitzak Gal and Myer Silverstone discussing the old,
outstanding debt. June 2000 photo by the author.

Only once during the evening did a Silverstone connect with a Gal. Myer Silverstone approached Yitzak Gal,
introduced himself and said, "Fifty years ago my father
loaned your uncle fifty-dollars, and now I'm here to collect."

Yitzak replied, "You've waited fifty years, you can wait
another fifty."

And the Silverstone-Gal family connection was never
accomplished.

In June 2004 there was another 'small world' occurrence.
Len and I were dinner guests at the Gal's family home in
Rosh Ha'ayin, Israel. During the evening, my cousin, Rami
Gal, gave Len a business card with his email address. The
following night, we attended a Silverstone wedding. We were
talking with my cousin, Judy Silverstone Godot, and she

wanted to give us her email address. Len had taken out Rami Gal's business card to write Judy's email information when her eyes caught the name on the card. Incredulous, Judy asked, "How do you know Rami Gal?"

We told her that he was our relative. Judy Silverstone Godot was stunned! She and Rami had been working together for the past two years and never knew that they, too, were related.

When I was pregnant with my first child in the 1960's, I informed Rabbi Harry that if the baby was a boy, I would *not* be having a Brit Milah / Bris, the circumcision of the male baby. This is considered the oldest rite in the Jewish religion and usually held on the eighth day of a healthy baby boy's life. I had signed papers for my obstetrician to perform the circumcision in the hospital and planned to have a naming party in the near future. Needless to say, Rabbi Harry was not pleased. Years later, when my decision came up for discussion, Rabbi Harry turned to me and calmly stated, "That is why you have three girls."

Shabbos Goy is the Hebrew and Yiddish term for a non-Jewish person who is hired by an orthodox/observant family to carry out specific activities that Jewish people are not permitted to do on the Sabbath. Jewish people always seem to find a way to get around the rules. One afternoon, our oldest daughter Jill, then about five years old, was having lunch at her best friend Cathy Reilly's house. Cathy happened to be Catholic and her father was older than most of the fathers in our neighborhood. Jill started talking about her grandmother, Mirm, being the youngest of ten children. Cathy's father, Mr. Reilly, then asked if her last name had been Silverstone. "Yes," replied Jill, astonished that Mr. Reilly would know that fact. "And I," said Mr. Reilly, "was their *Shabbos Goy!*"

In 1991, Rabbi Harry, Rebitzen Gertrude, Mirm, Judy and Len White met for dinner. Several minutes later, Mirm's very pregnant granddaughter, Jill White Richmond, and her husband, Kyle, joined us. As Jill sat down next to Rabbi Harry, he reached over, looked deeply into her eyes and said, "You are going to have a boy."

Jill was stunned as she had no idea what the gender of her baby would be. Jill asked her Uncle Harry how he knew and he replied it was a secret. Sure enough, six weeks later, Jill and Kyle's son, Aaron Samuel, joined the growing family of Silverstones.

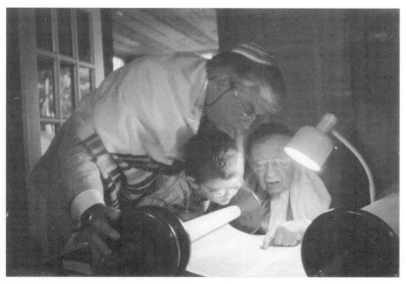

Leonard A. White, grandson Aaron Samuel Richmond and Rabbi Harry. Torah Reading during a High Holiday Service at Beth Gedaliah, 1995. (Photo by the author.)

Rabbi Harry let everyone know that his goal in life was to outlive George Burns, the actor, whose goal was to live to be 100. The two men had similar physical characteristics. In the movie *Oh God*, George Burns played "God" and another character in the movie was a Rabbi who was called "Rabbi Silverstone."

As he intended, Rabbi Harry lived to celebrate his **100th** birthday. On August 4, 1996, the Silverstone family and Beth Gedaliah Congregants, gathered to celebrate Rabbi Harry's 100th Birthday. When the Rabbi was asked what his secret was for living such a long life, his words of wisdom were, "It's not the years in your life but the life in your years." The last Silverstone family photograph was taken and everyone in the picture is a direct Silverstone relative. Husbands, wives, and extended family members were excluded from this photograph.

The Silverstone Family, 1996

May the Silverstone *mishagos* continue forever...

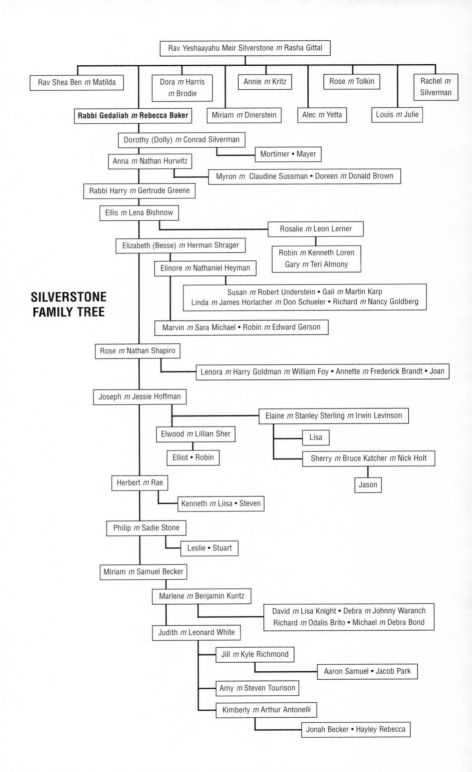

SILVERSTONE FAMILY TREE

Silverstone Family in Washington, D.C., circa 1950

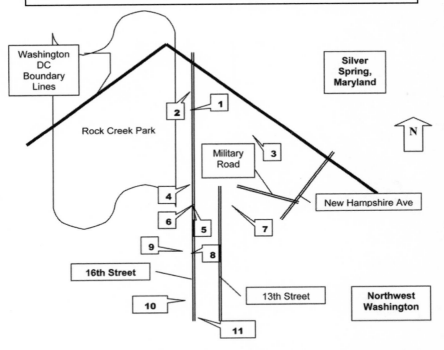

Washington DC Boundary Lines

Silver Spring, Maryland

N

Rock Creek Park

Military Road

New Hampshire Ave

16th Street

13th Street

Northwest Washington

1. Current Tifereth Israel Synagogue 7701-16th St. N.W.

2. Harry & Gertrude 7738-16th St. N.W.

3. Joseph & Jessie 709 Somerset Pl. N.W.

4. Miriam & Samuel 5713-16th St. N.W.

5. Rose & Nathan 5024-16th St. N.W.

6. Philip & Sadie 5018-16th St. N.W.

7. Herbert & Rae 5018- 16th St. N.W.

8. Besse Shrager Woodner Apts., 16th St. N.W.

9. Anna & Nathan 4122-18th St. N.W.

10. Ellis & Lena 1816 Ontario Pl. N.W.

11. Original Tifereth Israel Synagogue 14th & Euclid St. N.W.

(Dolly & Conrad London, England)

GLOSSARY

aliah – (Hebrew) To go up; the privilege of being called to the Torah, reserved strictly in orthodox theology to males over thirteen years of age who have become a bar mitzvah.

bar mitzvah – (Hebrew) The coming of age, a Jewish male, age thirteen or older, vows to follow the moral and ethical teachings of Judaism and Jewish traditions.

Beth (or bet) – (Hebrew) House of...

brit milah – (Hebrew) The oldest, continuous religious ritual; the ceremony of circumcision. Also referred to as a B'ris (Yiddish).

challah – (Hebrew) Braided egg bread used for Sabbath dinners and other holidays.

Haggadah – (Hebrew) The prayer book used during the Passover Seders.

kashruth – (Hebrew) Following the Jewish dietary laws of morality and hygiene.

ketubah – (Hebrew) Jewish marriage license.

kiddush – (Hebrew) The wine or juice that accompanies a prayer.

kosher – (Hebrew) Food selected and prepared according to Jewish Law, based on hygiene and morality.

Messiah – (English) Descendant of the House of David, the expected deliverer of the Jewish people.

michayah – (Hebrew) Relief; a good thing.

mishagos – (Yiddish) Nonsense, foolishness, craziness.

mitzvot – (Hebrew) Good deeds.

Pesach – (Hebrew) The holiday of Passover, celebrating the Jewish people's exodus from Israel to the promised land (Palestine/Israel).

Rabbi – (English) Teacher and leader of Jewish law, philosophy and tradition.

seder – (Hebrew) Order; also the evening meal and ritual commemorating the Passover holiday.

shabbat – (Hebrew) The Sabbath; Jewish day of rest and reflection.

Shabbos goy – (Yiddish) A non-Jewish person hired by orthodox families to carry-out activities which are forbidden for Jewish people to do on the Sabbath, such as turning lights off and on and lighting fires for heating and cooking.

shadchen – (Yiddish) A matchmaker; a marriage broker.

shehechiyanu – (Hebrew) Prayer of thanks.

shlogen kapores – (Yiddish) The Jewish ritual of waving a live chicken over one's head to transfer the sins of the person to the chicken at the time of the Yom Kippur holiday.

shul – (Yiddish) Temple, synagogue, house of worship.

simcha – (Hebrew, noun) A good thing; a celebration.

sukot – (Hebrew) The fall season holiday celebrated by building a booth and thanking God for the harvest.

Talmud – (Hebrew) The most famous collection of Jewish teachings assembled over the years from the third to the seventh centuries. Discourse and literary argument of the Sages contained in 26 volumes.

Torah – (Hebrew) The Teachings; written oral history comprising the Five Books of Moses that are the foundation of Jewish law.

traif – (Yiddish) Not kosher.

tush – (Yiddish) Backside.

tzedakah – (Hebrew) Charity.

Yeshiva – (Hebrew) An institution dedicated to the education of higher learning in Jewish theology.